PAPERBACK **PLUS**

Contents

Meet the Authors

Zheng Zhensun

Zheng Zhensun is a journalist and photographer who has traveled all over China, the United States, Canada, and Southeast Asia covering news stories. He works as a senior journalist at the Xinhua News Agency in Beijing, China. Zheng Zhensun was invited by New China Pictures, Xinhua's affiliate, to write *A Young Painter* and to take the photographs of Wang Yani and her paintings that appear in the book.

Zheng Zhensun with Wang Yani.

Alice Low

Alice Low majored in art history at Smith College, and has written many books for children of all ages. One of her books, *The Macmillan Book of Greek Gods and Heroes*, won the Washington Irving Children's Choice Award for nonfiction (1988). She has also reviewed children's books in the *New York Times*, been editor of Children's Choice Book Club and has taught art and creative writing to children.

Alice Low with her granddaughter, Maggie.

A Young Painter

A Young Painter

The life and paintings
of Wang Yani —
China's extraordinary
young artist

by Zheng Zhensun and Alice Low

Photographs by Zheng Zhensun
Introduction by Jan Stuart

HOUGHTON MIFFLIN COMPANY
BOSTON
ATLANTA   DALLAS   GENEVA, ILLINOIS   PALO ALTO   PRINCETON

Acknowledgments

For each of the selections listed below, grateful acknowledgment is made for permission to excerpt and/or reprint original or copyrighted materials, as follows:

Selections

"Animal Scribbles," from *Draw!*, by Kim Solga. Copyright © 1991 by F&W Publications. Reprinted by permission of North Light Books, a division of F&W Publications.

"Animals in Art," by Marjorie Jackson, from April 1994 *Cricket* magazine, Vol. XXI, No. 8. Copyright © 1994 by Marjorie Jackson. Reprinted by permission of *Cricket* magazine. Cover art copyright © 1994 by Leslie H. Morrill. Reprinted by permission of the artist.

A Young Painter: The Life and Painting of Wang Yani, China's Extraordinary Young Artist, by Zhensun Zheng and Alice Low. Copyright © 1991 by Byron Preiss Visual Publications. Reprinted by permission.

Photography

82 Scala/Art Resource (t); Asian Art Museum of San Francisco, The Avery Brundage Collection B60B1+ (b). **83** ©British Museum (t).
84 Werner Forman Archive, Hermitage Museum/Art Resource.
85 Courtesy of Leo Mildenberg Collection, Zurich, photo by Silvia Hertig, Archaologische Sammlung der Universitat Zurich. **86** Bridgeman/Art Resource (m). **87** Emille Museum. **88** ©1994 Artist's Rights Society (ARS), New York/SPADEM, Paris (t); Courtesy Inuit Art Section DIANA (Dept. of Indian and Northern Affairs Canada) (b). **89** Edward Thorpe Gallery (t)

Houghton Mifflin Edition, 1996

Printed in the U.S.A.

ISBN: 0-395-73268-9

23456789-B-99 98 97 96 95

Contents

Introduction

A friendly but quiet girl, Yani often prefers to communicate her thoughts in painting instead of by speaking. Once, when Yani was hungry, she painted a baby monkey eating fruit. She showed this to her mother instead of directly asking for a snack. When Yani had her first inoculation, she painted a wide-eyed little monkey who expressed Yani's own struggle to be brave at the doctor's office. She called the painting *I Am Not Scared*.

Most children have imaginary playmates like young Wang Yani did. But her skill and discipline in translating them into paintings is rare. Now that Yani is an adolescent, she paints fewer "stories" of playful animals. Instead, she concentrates on the landscape and people around her.

No matter whether Yani paints frolicking animals or a quiet landscape, her paintings always have a rhythmic energy. When you look at her paintings, it is easy to imagine the sweeping movements she made with her brush, ink and colors. The Chinese admire vigorous brushstrokes that allow the viewer to mentally re-create the artist's process of painting. Yani has given new authority to the Chinese saying that "the brush sings and the ink dances" in a good painting. In fact, Wang Yani herself loves to dance. Such physical training is important to her performance as a painter. And she often listens to music while she paints. Thus for Yani, music, dance, and painting are related.

Wang Yani is largely self-taught. She was born with essential skills that an artist needs—a fertile imagination, a good memory, and quick reflexes. Yani sometimes starts a painting with a blank mind. She dribbles a few dots of ink and responds to these with another brushstroke and then another,

A Game With a Wild Plant
Age 5
2 ft. 1 in. × 2 ft. 2 in.

until she weaves a clear picture from the ink blobs.

Wang Yani paints in a centuries-old tradition, but she continually delights us with a direct immediacy and freshness in her paintings.

Jan Stuart, Assistant Curator of Chinese Art, Arthur M. Sackler Gallery and Freer Gallery of Art, Smithsonian Institution, Washington, D.C.

Preface

In 1989, Wang Yani, a fourteen-year-old Chinese artist, traveled to Washington, D.C., for the opening of an exhibition of her paintings. Hundreds of thousands of visitors came to see her bold, energetic art in the Arthur M. Sackler Gallery of the Smithsonian Institution.

The exhibition was called, "Yani: The Brush of Innocence," for Yani had painted many of the pictures of animals, birds, and landscapes when she was between the ages of three and eleven years old.

Yani, who is now twenty, has painted more than ten thousand pictures. When she was four years old, her paintings were exhibited in the Chinese cities of Beijing, Shanghai and Guangzhou. A painting by four-year-old Yani was even reproduced on a postage stamp. It was of a monkey, and it was called *Scratching an Itch for Mother.*

Yani gives a painting demonstration at the exhibition of her paintings in Washington, D.C.

Below:
Don't Fight!   *Age 6*
1 ft. 1½ in. × 4 ft. 3½ in.
In this painting, the monkey, who represents Yani, helps settle a quarrel between two roosters. The roosters represent other children in Yani's neighborhood.

8

Above:
Scratching an Itch for Mother
Age 4
Actual size.
Yani's painting was made into a postage stamp and issued in China when she was eight years old.

Since the age of ten, Yani has held solo exhibitions in Japan, Hong Kong, Germany, the United States, and Great Britain. Everywhere, people are amazed at this outpouring of highly original, beautiful painting done by an artist so young.

Yani has not been pushed or taught to paint. Quite simply, she loves to paint. For Yani, painting is both an amusement and a passion, and she never gets bored with it. Yani loves to paint every day to record her thoughts and feelings, much as people record their daily thoughts in diaries.

"I think painting is something very simple," says Yani. "You just paint what you think about. You don't have to follow any instruction. Everybody can paint."

Yani's paintings express the thoughts and feelings of an unusually talented young person who grew up in a small town in China.

Zheng Zhensun and Alice Low

Collection of the artist

Growing Up in Gongcheng

Wang Yani was born and grew up in the small town of Gongcheng, which is in the Guangxi Zhuang Autonomous Region of southern China. This is a beautiful area with green hills, clear blue rivers, and ancient temples. Not far away are the famous cone-shaped, rugged mountains of Guilin, which have an unreal, fairy-tale quality, especially when they are shrouded in mist and clouds.

Gongcheng County in the Guangxi Zhuang Autonomous Region.

Next door to Yani's home in Gongcheng was a Confucian temple where lovely flowers bloomed. In front of the house there was a lotus pond, and the Chaijiang River, full of fish, flowed nearby. Yani and her younger brother, Wang Xiangyu, often played by the river. They floated boats in it, waded across it, or went rafting. Yani liked to take a stroll along the riverbank every day.

Yani and her brother also walked their dog on a nearby hill, which was covered with pine and camphor trees. In the spring and summer, this same hill was dotted with wild flowers. When Yani was a little child, her father often carried her on his

Yani loves the beautiful countryside of Gongcheng County.

A bird's-eye view of Gongcheng County. The clear blue Chaijiang River surrounds the county on three sides.

Mountain in Rain
Age 8
1 ft. 1 in. × 1 ft. 1½ in.
The mountains of Guilin have an unreal, fairy-tale quality, especially when they are shrouded in mist and clouds.

shoulders, and together they roamed the mountains and the riverbanks.

Growing up with all this beauty around her has had a tremendous influence on Yani. She is interested in all of nature—in the sun, the moon, mountains, rivers, fish, flowers, trees, birds, and animals

11

Left: The white house next to the Confucian temple was Yani's home in Gongcheng.
Right: Yani goes rafting with her brother.

of all kinds. Animals are of particular interest to Yani, and she has always had a pet to play with — including a cat, a dog, and even a monkey, which her father gave her when she was four years old. Yani called her pet monkey Lida and has taken care of her ever since. When she was very young, Yani would spend day after day playing with Lida and singing songs to her.

"Get to your seat," Yani used to tell Lida, "and we'll eat candies together. One for you and one for me."

Yani loved monkeys so much that she painted hundreds of pictures of them. In fact, she often thought of herself and her brother as monkeys. One of Yani's favorite pictures is a scroll painting called *A Hundred Monkeys.* Yani explains that in it she has included herself as a monkey playing with Wang Xiangyu.

"He likes to be tickled, so in that painting I'm tickling him," she says.

This painting is very large (approximately 12 inches by 35 feet) and in four hours Yani had

Above:
Let's Go and Pick Fruit
Age 7
1 ft. 1 in. × 1 ft. 1½ in.
Yani paints animals she has seen in real life. In this painting, a monkey rides on the back of a water buffalo.

Right: Yani meets some water buffalo when she goes swimming.

painted 112 monkeys in various postures and with different expressions on their faces. If she had had more time, Yani would have painted even more monkeys!

Yani remembers everything she sees, because she has a keen sense of observation. She never paints directly from life, but from memory instead. Yani doesn't paint everything realistically as she remembers it, however. She puts her own ideas and feelings about what she has observed into her paintings.

For example, one day, when she was four, Yani painted a tree without leaves, and the fruit was attached to the tree trunk. When her father asked her why there were no leaves on the tree, Yani

Detail from A Hundred Monkeys
Age 9
The whole painting is 35 feet long and shows 112 monkeys in various postures and with different expressions on their faces.

14

Yani buys fruit and vegetables with her mother in the farmers' market.

answered simply, "Leaves are not edible. Why should I have them on my tree?"

Yani has a warm, loving family. Her mother, Tang Fenjiao, works in the toy department of a store. Yani has always loved going shopping with her mother, and they often go to the farmers' market together to pick out fruit and vegetables. Though Yani's family name is Wang, and her brother has the same name, their mother has kept her family name of Tang, as is the custom for married women in China.

In traditional Chinese life, the father of the family is very important and is responsible for all major decisions. Yani's father, Wang Shiqiang, is an art educator as well as a painter who excels in

15

Yani's family is preparing a meal. Yani helps her mother to make "oil tea," a speciality of Gongcheng. The tea is boiled with ginger and lard.

oil painting. He has done something extraordinary in stressing freedom and spontaneity in Yani's art; traditional Chinese education, including art education of children, has emphasized uniformity rather than individuality. Yani's father says that neither he nor his artist friends have taught Yani to paint. When Yani started "scribbling" at the age of two and a half, he encouraged her to continue in her own way, without interfering. From that time on, Yani painted daily, and she has continued to do so, usually completing about three paintings a day.

Yani often paints after school and before she goes to bed. When she was younger, and her mother told her to stop painting because it was bedtime, Yani would call back that she wanted to do just one more painting.

Yani spent a lot of time at home until she was about four. Therefore, many of her early monkey paintings show the love between parents and their children. By the time she was five or six, Yani had more opportunity to play with other children, and her paintings from that time began to include birds and animals representing other children at play.

Opposite top:
I Want to Play
Age 4
1 ft. 1½ in. × 1 ft. 1½ in.
Many of Yani's early paintings show the love between parents and their children.

Opposite bottom
Fish
Age 6
1 ft. 1 in. × 4 ft. 4½ in.
Yani paints many colorful paintings. Here, she was inspired by living near the Chaijiang River which is full of fish.

She painted roosters chasing each other; peacocks dancing; and monkeys riding on a deer, a crane, or a camel.

At the age of seven Yani entered the Shiyan Primary School in Gongcheng. Then as now, she enjoyed school, got along well with her classmates, and made many friends. Today, Yani also loves sports and games, but this was not always so. When Yani was a young child, she was a little shy and afraid of being alone. This is reflected in her paintings of that period—tiny flowers and grass are painted with weak brushstrokes; the animals are quiet and still. Her father and his friends, also painters, noticed this and decided to help Yani overcome her timidness.

They taught Yani to swim and play games and climb hills and run. They also encouraged her to rid herself of her stage fright when she met crowds at her exhibitions.

One day, Yani heard from her friends that the Confucian temple next to her house was haunted. Yani was so scared that she did not dare leave her house for several evenings. So her father, who

Playing basketball. After school, Yani plays basketball, Ping-Pong, or goes jogging with friends.

Yani and her classmates have a picnic.

18

Let's Go for a Game
Age 5
2 ft. 2 in. × 2 ft. 2 in.
When Yani was five, she started playing more with other children. The animals and birds in her paintings represent children at play.

noticed that she had a problem, took Yani to play in the temple until she was convinced that there were no ghosts there. Through her father's encouragement, Yani finally went to the temple alone. Soon she liked to play there with her friends. As time went by, Yani became brave, sometimes naughty, and always imaginative.

Another way that Yani's father encouraged his daughter was to give her big brushes and large sheets of paper.

"This has helped my daughter overcome timidness in painting, and become bold," he says.

On Yani's twelfth birthday, she painted a huge picture and at the height of her enthusiasm, she scooped up some ink with her hands and poured it on the painting. She wanted to see the effect of the natural flow of ink on paper.

Today, Yani continues to be imaginative and inquisitive, and her paintings reflect her exuberance and love of life.

On her twelfth birthday Yani painted a huge picture and poured some ink on the painting. She wanted to see the effect of the natural flow of ink on paper.

20

Childhood
Age 10
1 ft. 6 in. × 6 ft.
Yani's style of
painting is
vigorous and bold.

From Scribbling to Painting

How did Yani progress from the toddler who loved to scribble to the outstanding painter that she has become at such a young age?

"Yani came into this world accompanied by the smell of paint and ink," says her father.

It all began when he took Yani, then age two and a half, to his studio. While he was busy painting, Yani picked up a piece of charcoal and began scribbling on the wall. Every now and then she moved back a little, tilted her head to one side, and squinted at her "masterpiece," obviously delighted with her mess of black circles and lines.

Her father did not scold her as some parents might have done. Instead, he encouraged her, saying, "Yani, you are great. Do you want to draw like Papa?" Then he handed her a pencil and sheets of paper and said, "Draw on the paper, Yani."

From that time on, Yani continued to "draw," although she was really scribbling. To Yani, drawing was a way of playing and using her imagination, and each picture had a story behind it.

Another day, Yani said to her father, "Papa, you always paint other people. Can you paint me, too?"

So her father put down his own work, took a piece of charcoal, and said, "Sit down and look at me!" Before long, he had finished his sketch. "Does it look like you?" he asked. "Yes!" said the little girl. Wang Shiqiang went back to his work again. But soon Yani came over to him and said in a serious voice, "Papa, let me draw a picture of *you*."

So Wang Shiqiang sat on a stool and modeled for Yani while she drew. When he did not look at her directly, she ordered, "Hi, look at me!"

When she was finished, she said to her father, "Does it look like you?" At first, her father laughed

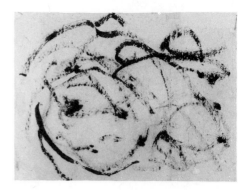

Age 2½   8 × 9 in.
Yani's first attempts were just scribbles.

Mountain and Bridge
Age 2½
9 × 11 in.
In Yani's early pictures, lines and shapes were often symbols for things she had seen in real life.

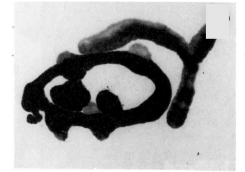

Cat
Age 2½
1 ft. 1 in. × 1 ft.
In a short time, Yani went from scribbling to painting.

Little Monkey
Age 3
5¾ × 6¼ in.
Same size as the original. When she was very young, Yani painted hundreds of pictures of monkeys.

because the sketch looked like a dozen or more earthworms crawling over a stone. But to please Yani, her father said, "Yes! Yes!"

Yani was so encouraged that, though still only two and a half, she sketched everyone she met, from children to older people.

But drawing on paper didn't interest Yani for long. Soon she wanted to use paints and brushes and paint on canvas the way her father did. One day, before Yani was three years old, she asked her father if she could paint on the oil painting he had been working on. Her father was taken aback. How could he let his little daughter paint on *his* painting? After some thought he came up with a solution. He handed Yani a clean brush without any paint on it.

So Yani painted on her father's painting, but her dry brush left no marks. When she was finished, it was clear that she could imagine some sort of picture she had made, for she said, "This is my painting!"

However, one day when her father was out, Yani mixed his oil paints herself and used them on her father's painting. When her father came home, of course he was angry at Yani for ruining a painting he had worked on for days. Wang Shiqiang hoped that his show of anger would stop Yani from painting on his work.

So Yani cried and cried, for she thought her father would punish her. After a while, she stopped crying, tugged at her father's sleeve and said, "Papa, I was helping you paint. I want to paint and paint."

Yani's father was amazed at her words. He wiped

Yani, age four, painting. Yani paints with the brushes, ink, and pigment used in traditional Chinese painting.

24

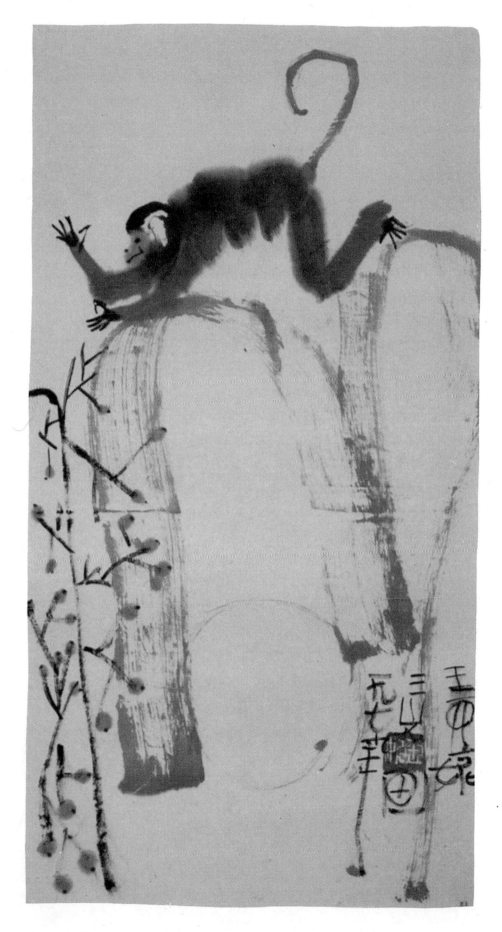

I Want Fruit
Age 3
1 ft. 1 in. × 2 ft. 2 in.
Yani's imagination is one of her strengths. It helps her to paint lively and original paintings.

her tears away and thought to himself, "Is this child born to paint?"

Wang Shiqiang recognized his daughter's talent. But, he wondered, what was the best way for him to help her develop it? How should he begin?

Yani's father does not believe that children should learn to paint by copying other artists. Nor does he believe they should be told how or what to paint. This would stifle their imagination.

"We should encourage children to think and paint by themselves," he says. "Adults should never interfere and do things for them because we do not have the innocent minds children have." Wang Shiqiang values the importance of young children's feelings and understands that they have different ways of seeing the world.

Her father tells this story. One day, he and Yani were strolling along the riverbank when Yani suddenly stopped. She picked up a pebble and examined it carefully before putting it in her pocket. Then she squatted on the ground, picking up pebble after pebble.

"What are you going to do with all those pebbles?" her father asked.

"See," said Yani, "this one is a monkey. Look at its eyes, nostrils, and mouth."

"I see," said her father. "And what is this one?"

"This is an old monkey feeding a baby monkey. Look, it is putting a finger into the baby monkey's mouth."

Yani's father was delighted that she could "see" lively monkeys in ordinary stones. What an imaginative child! No wonder the monkeys she painted were becoming more and more lifelike.

One rainy day, Yani said to him, "Papa, please write a letter to the sun for me. Ask it to come out right away. I want to play outdoors."

26

"How can I command the sun?" her father asked.

"I can," said Yani. "I can command both the sun and the moon because they always follow me wherever I happen to be."

Wang Shiqiang laughed, but he wasn't laughing *at* his daughter. Rather, he was delighted at Yani's fanciful way of thinking.

Another time, Yani painted a tree bearing two kinds of fruit. Her father asked her, "Is there such a tree in this world?"

Yani replied right away, "There certainly is. It is called the Strange Tree." Yani had painted a tree that could bear the two kinds of fruit she liked best.

In 1978, when Yani was three years old, her father took her on an exciting train trip to the city of Nanning, about 375 miles from their home in Gongcheng.

The reason for the journey was that Wang Shiqiang had been invited to Nanning to work on an oversized painting for the Guangxi Museum.

Wang Shiqiang had wanted to take Yani with him, and while he was considering this idea, some of his painter friends called to urge him to bring her. They wanted to meet this young child who had such a flair for painting. So it was decided. All the adults were happy that Yani was coming to Nanning, but none of them knew that this trip was going to be such an important step — the first leg of the long journey Yani was to take into the world of painting.

When Yani and her father arrived at the museum, Yani said, "Papa, I want to paint right away." Her father, who had been a little worried about how he would paint and baby-sit at the same time, was delighted at her request. He said, "Tomorrow,

Yani, age three, in Nanning City.

Opposite:
Plum Blossom
Age 4
1 ft. 1 in. × 4 ft. 3 in.
*Yani paints things she loves,
among them, flowers.*

after I have unpacked my paints and canvases, you will have lots of time for painting. Papa will paint here, in this studio, and you will paint right next to me and not go anywhere else."

The next day, Yani began painting next to her father, but when he became totally absorbed in his painting, Yani sneaked out. For, although her father had said not to go anywhere, he had left the door open, and Yani was curious. She wanted to see the other painters at work in the other studios.

Day after day, Yani went from studio to studio. She loved watching the other painters working. Because she was the only child there, she became the darling of the painters, and she got along well with them. When they wanted to take a break, they would stop and joke with her or play hide-and-seek.

These painters also gave her lots of paper and brushes, but none of them tried to teach her to paint. They thought that a three-year-old's doodling was just child's play.

But Yani took her drawing and painting very seriously. It was so exciting being with all these professional painters! When she was painting, she forgot everything else—even playing with her friends or being with the rest of her family. She was completely focused on painting, and soon the lower part of the studio wall was covered with her "masterpieces."

Three-year-old Yani painted birds, animals, houses, the sun, and children. At first, the forms she painted were symbols for these things, but as the weeks went by, the forms Yani painted became easier to recognize. When she pointed to a tree in her painting, people saw that it looked like one.

Yani was growing, and her painting abilities were growing, too.

Yani, age five, painting in her studio at home.

Cat
Age 3
4½ × 8½ in.
Same size as the original.
In this painting, Yani
captures the feeling of the
way a cat moves.

3

Monkeys, Monkeys, Monkeys

Something else new and interesting happened to three-year-old Yani during her stay in Nanning. Her father took her to the Nanning Zoo, and Yani was completely smitten with the playful monkeys. She jumped and shouted with joy when she saw them for the first time. She loved to imitate their actions, too, blinking her eyes when they blinked theirs, making faces as they made faces at her, and shrieking and running as they shrieked and ran. She even pleaded to go into their cages to play with them. She watched the monkeys for hours and hours, and cried when it was time to go home.

The playful monkeys left a deep impression on Yani. When she and her father returned home, he asked her, "What are you going to paint today?" Yani imitated a monkey and answered, without hesitation, "Monkeys!"

From that time on, Yani painted hundreds of pictures of monkeys.

At first, Yani's monkeys had whiskers and walked on all fours. She had painted so many pictures of cats that she couldn't see all the differences between the two animals. So, whenever her father's friends had time, they would take Yani to the zoo and point out how they differed.

Yani observed the monkeys closely, and after a while, the monkeys she painted looked more like real ones. Yani painted monkeys scratching their ears, fighting for fruits, playing games, or sleeping.

However, these paintings were not detailed or realistic. They were Yani's *impressions* of the monkeys she saw and remembered.

Since Yani's feelings and thoughts were always in the process of change as she grew, Yani's monkey paintings changed, too. Soon *her* monkeys

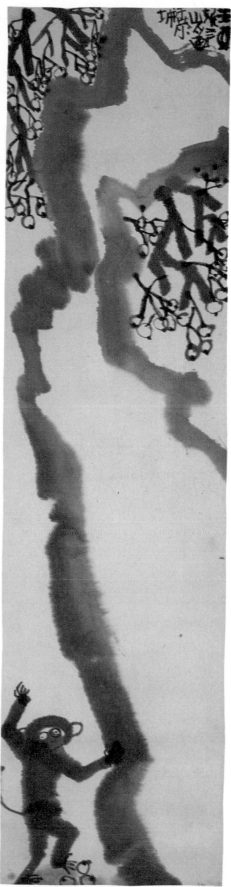

*Yani's paintings
often have stories
behind them.*

Right:
Is There a Moon
on the Water?
Age 4
1 ft. 1 in. × 4 ft. 3 in.

Far right:
Who Picked the Fruit?
Age 4
1 ft. 1 in. × 4 ft. 3 in.

Above:
Kitten
Age 3
6 × 8 in.
*Yani painted cats before she
painted monkeys.*

Left:
Little Monkey
Age 3
6 × 7½ in.
*The monkey looks more like a cat
because Yani had not yet seen all the
differences between the two animals.*

Opposite:
Monkey
Age 3
6¾ × 9 in.
Same size as the original.
*Little by little, Yani's monkeys looked
more like the real ones.*

11·8

30

were not just like the real monkeys she saw; they were monkeys of her imagination, and their personalities were often like herself—cheerful and fanciful, with her own feelings. Yani's monkeys could cry, play the *erhu* (a Chinese string instrument) or play hide-and-seek and tug-of-war.

In fact, Yani grew to like them more than her pet monkey, Lida. One day, she said to her father, "I don't like Lida anymore."

"Why?" asked her father.

"Because Lida is not as cute as the monkeys I paint," said Yani. "They can talk, tell stories, steal fruit, make jokes, and perform acrobatics. But Lida can't. She stares at me with open eyes like a fool when I tell her stories."

Yani, age five, with one of her paintings. Yani's paintings can sometimes be larger than she is! Here, the monkeys are as playful as the real ones Yani saw in Nanning Zoo.

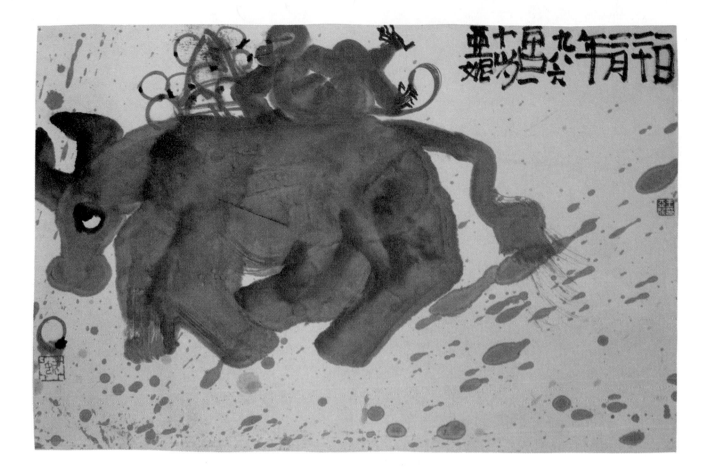

Going Home
Age 10
1 ft. 6 in. × 2 ft. 3 in.
In this painting an ox helps the monkey to get home.

Who Picked the Fruit?, a little monkey is looking up at a tree hoping for fruit, but the fruit is gone.

Yani's monkeys are often mischievous, like herself, her brother, or other children. In her painting *Talking Quietly*, two monkeys are squatting near some bright flowers. The baby monkey is whispering into the ear of the older one. "The little one is urging the old monkey to steal the flowers," explains Yani.

In *Going Home*, Yani explains that a monkey is so busy looking for fruit that he gets lost. Luckily, an ox comes along, and gives him a ride all the way home!

Yani's experiences of things she has seen and felt in real life are reflected in her monkey paintings, too. For example, Yani painted *Carrying the*

Sedan Chair after she had seen brides in her town being carried to their new husbands' homes. This is an ancient Chinese custom. In this painting, as in others, Yani uses animals in the place of people.

One day, Yani's father bought her a red umbrella. She was hoping it would rain, but no rain came. So Yani painted a little monkey holding an umbrella and playing happily in the rain.

Above:
Detail from
Carrying the Sedan Chair
Age 6
9 in. x 4 ft. 5 in.

Opposite:
Little Monkeys and Mummy
Age 5
1 ft. 3 in. × 1 ft. 9 in.
Yani spent a lot of time watching monkeys closely. In this painting Yani has captured the lively antics of the monkeys.

Above:
At Little Monkey's Home
Age 7
2 ft. 2 in. × 2 ft. 2 in.
Later, Yani's monkeys came from her imagination and they could do anything she wanted them to.

Opposite:
Having a Swing
Age 9
1 ft. 3 in. × 1 ft. 6 in.
Yani's monkeys like to play the same games that Yani played with her friends.

4
How Yani Paints

Like many other people, Yani started to draw by doodling dots and lines. But in less than a year, she passed that stage of early childhood drawing, a stage that most children take years to get through. Yani also mastered the art of using brush and ink when she was a very young child. At the age of three, while other children could barely draw recognizable figures, she was painting her pictures of lively cats and monkeys.

Yani's paintings are fresh, vigorous, and bold. A Japanese artist, Yikuo Hiyayama, commented on the works Yani painted at this early age. He said they were "solid in structure, with smooth brushwork, and clear lines." He said they did not have any unnecessary polishing, for Yani had known just what to omit, and he also stated that she knew how to use the paper in a way that would bring out its ability to soak up paint.

Yani holds her brush in different ways according to the size of the brush and the way she thinks is best for her. Once, when Yani's schoolteacher wanted her to hold the brush in a way that was unnatural to her, Yani's father interfered. He encouraged Yani to go back to holding the brush in her own way.

Yani's father has also advised her never to fix her eyes on the tip of the brush as she paints, but to scan the whole sheet of paper and even beyond it so as to have a wide field of vision. As time has gone by, Yani's brushstrokes have become more powerful. Now, with a few rapid sweeps of the brush and a soft twist of her wrist, Yani swiftly paints an old green tree and adds a tail to a monkey.

Yani handles the brush with ease, sometimes painting swiftly, sometimes slowly, sometimes

When she was young Yani used to sing, dance, chat and make faces while she was painting.

cleverly, sometimes bluntly, and sometimes unevenly. She also uses ink in different ways—dry, moist, strong and light—to create different effects.

When Yani was very young, she could not concentrate on her painting as deeply as she does now. She used to leave her painting to play after doing only a few brushstrokes. Sometimes while painting she sang, danced, chatted, made faces, and even imitated other people and animals.

Now that Yani is older, she approaches her painting a little differently. Before she paints, she calms herself to clear her mind and then waits for inspiration. But when she starts painting, she does not know exactly what she will paint. The idea develops as she works. Yani likes to listen to music on her Walkman while she paints. She believes that music stimulates her feelings. Her favorite music is Beethoven's Fifth Symphony and works by Schubert and Mozart, as well as Chinese music.

Below left: Yani clears her mind before starting to paint. Below center: Listening to music on her Walkman helps Yani paint. Below right: Careful brushwork.

Yani's father never comments on his daughter's work in her presence, for he doesn't want her to paint according to *his* likes and dislikes. Nor does he expect her to do perfect work. In his opinion, if he were to consider her work to be perfect, her imaginative ideas would probably dry up. He wants Yani, the child artist, to keep searching for ways to push her experiences and knowledge forward.

Yani never does any copying, nor does she paint from life. She remembers everything she sees, and she paints her lively pictures completely from memory. One example of her amazing visual memory occurred when, as a young child, Yani asked her father to write some words for her to copy. Yani's father did not want her to copy his way of writing Chinese characters, so he wrote them in the air with his fingers. Yani watched his movements very carefully and proceeded to write the characters on paper, just as her father had drawn them.

Yani's father encourages Yani to remember what she has seen during the day and to paint what has affected her the most. He has always stressed that Yani should paint her impressions of the things she has seen, rather than concentrating on the details and special features. That is why there are no peaks in Yani's paintings of beautiful Guilin. Instead, she has painted her overall impressions that the Guilin landscape has left in her mind.

Likewise, though Yani's monkeys are very lively and have all the traits of these mischievous animals, none of them is painted true to form. They are the products of her impressions after her many trips to the zoo. Some of their gestures are simply from Yani's imagination. Instead of reproducing their actual behavior, Yani let her monkeys reflect her own feelings about them.

Above:
Animals' Autumn
Age 14
3 ft. 2 in. × 5 ft. 10½ in.
(Painted in Washington, D.C.)
Yani's inscription tells how autumn is a time when trees wither, but when animals are happy because there is plenty of food for them to eat.

Opposite:
Let Me Get to the Bank
Age 6
1 ft 1 in. × 4 ft. 4 in.
Yani's paintings are full of life. In this painting she captures the movement of fish swimming and of a monkey swinging on branches above the water.

Her first monkeys were without hair or toes, but her father did not point this out to her because he knew that his small daughter had to pass through a certain process before becoming familiar with her subject. He knew that Yani would make changes in the way she painted the monkeys within the natural course of time. Though Yani did give her monkeys hair and toes as she grew older, her monkeys were still not painted in great detail. They were Yani's overall impression of monkeys.

When Yani was eight years old, her father made a painful personal decision in order to further protect his daughter's originality and creativity. He quit painting altogether, even though he was rising to the peak of his career. His oil paintings were shown at every art exhibition in Guangxi, and the largest one, *Liberate Guangxi,* was in the collection of the regional museum.

Why did he cut short his painting career? The

43

reason was that he was afraid his style of painting, using oils rather than Chinese brush and ink, would have a poor effect on Yani, who painted with traditional Chinese materials and used many of the traditional Chinese brushstrokes.

Wang Shiqiang's friends have asked him if

Nursing
Age 6
1 ft. 1 in. × 1 ft. 1 in.
Yani shows the love between a mother monkey and her baby.

44

Mountain in Spring
Age 8
1 ft. × 1 ft. 1 in.
Yani paints her impressions of the things she has seen rather than concentrating on the details.

he feels sad about giving up his oil painting.

"Yes," he said, "but I see in Yani a more promising artist than Wang Shiqiang. I have a duty to help and protect her so that she will use her artistic talents fully." He added that he hopes to go back to his own painting when Yani turns eighteen.

5

Yani and Her Father

Though Wang Shiqiang has protected Yani's creativity and freedom to express herself, he has also furnished her with guidance and stimulation, and he has done everything possible to create an atmosphere that would lead to her artistic growth.

Not only did he introduce her to the beauties of nature while she was very young, but he also took her to interesting places, which stimulated her mind.

After Yani was four, she went with her father to many cities where her work was exhibited, and so she had many wonderful experiences. She climbed the Taishan Mountains and the Great Wall, visited the Palace Museum in Beijing and the Confucian temple in Qufu, Shandong Province. In recent years she has toured many countries, and these trips have expanded her knowledge and broadened her artistic approach.

And though Yani's father has been cautious about giving advice to Yani, he has helped to strengthen her understanding of the things she has seen.

For instance, one day a botanist visited the Wang family, and Yani's father asked him to talk about the function of leaves, for Yani had painted trees without leaves. Yani listened to the botanist speak, and the next day, Yani's painting showed leaves on a tree. On the tip of each leaf hung a fruit. Yani also said, "Monkeys eat fruit, and fruit eat leaves." This was *her* understanding of the botanist's explanation of how leaves get their food. Though she could not absorb all of the facts, she was making progress. Soon after that, Wang Shiqiang took Yani to an orchard, where she saw that fruit grew on twigs.

Since then, Yani has painted many paintings of

Yani, age six, painting in Beijing.

Opposite:
The Ripe Fruit
Age 12
1 ft. 1 in. × 4 ft. 5 in.
Yani paints fruit hanging from twigs not from leaves as she used to do when she was much younger.

trees and fruit, and the fruit hangs from twigs, not from leaves!

Yani's father has helped her to see pictures in her mind by encouraging her to make up stories. When Yani was five, he took her to Guangzhou on a ship. Wang Shiqiang started telling Yani a story, then Yani responded with one of her own. To the astonishment of the passengers, the two of them told each other stories for seven hours!

Yani's father has also encouraged her to think independently and to solve problems by herself. In the Wangs' courtyard there is a hibiscus tree, which bears white flowers in the morning and red in the evening. Yani painted a picture and called it, *Hibiscus Flowers Are White in the Morning*. She painted the petals in a very light color and showed the painting to her father. "Doesn't this look beautiful?" she asked.

"Is this white?" asked Wang Shiqiang, for the petals looked quite gray.

Yani thought for a moment. Then she took her brush, dipped it in thick black ink, and painted the background dark. In contrast, the petals now looked white. Yani's father thought so, too, and nodded his head in approval.

Wang Shiqiang frequently created problems for Yani while she was painting, in order to sharpen her mind and make her more visually sensitive. One day, Yani drew a horizontal line across a sheet of paper. When her father asked her what she was going to paint, she answered, "A bridge."

"A bridge is not pleasing to the eye," said her father. "Why not paint something else?"

Yani thought for a few moments. Then quickly, she transformed the line into a shoulder pole with a basket of fruit hanging from either end. She added a little monkey carrying it and hurrying along.

47

Yani and her father have made it a rule that she should never say, "I don't know," when he asks her a question, for there is always an answer to be found.

"When Yani was painting, I would pretend not to know anything about what she was after," said Wang Shiqiang. "Every time she would finish a painting, I would ask her why it was painted in that certain way; for example, why there was so much space left in the painting. Yani would never say, 'I don't know.' Instead, she would think about what I had asked." He added that if their views differed because of the difference in their ages, he would just say, "I don't necessarily agree with you." Sometimes, when Yani's painting didn't seem to make sense to him, he would praise her on purpose and even say, "It's wonderful." Then Yani would keep on painting enthusiastically, until she herself realized what a mess she had made.

When Yani's father treated her this way, his aim was to build up her thinking and creativity, rather than to let her mind drift. "Inspiration and guidance, when given in an appropriate way, are essential to protect and develop a child's ability to imagine and create," he says. He adds that it is important to keep that guidance within the boundaries of the child's stage of development.

Yani's father loves her very much, but he can be strict with her when necessary. He feels that a good artist must have a strong character; therefore, discipline is important.

As Yani became famous, she became proud, too, and sometimes she lost her temper. Her father and his friends were concerned about this.

When Yani was four and a half years old, she put on a painting demonstration in the city of Yangzhou. Somebody overturned a cup by accident

Right:
Two Little Friends
Age 11
1 ft. 2 in. × 2 ft. 3 in.
Yani shows that animals
have personalities.

Opposite:
Hibiscus Flowers Are
White in the Morning
Age 5
1 ft. 1 in. × 4 ft. 3 in.
Yani painted a dark
background to make the
petals look whiter.

and wet the table on which she was working. She went into a rage, flung her brush away, and sat fuming, tight-lipped. Soon she started to paint again, but she did it half-heartedly.

Afterwards, Yani and her father returned to the hotel room, and her father told her that if she wanted to continue to be a painter she must be serious, not temperamental and arrogant.

Yani promised to paint seriously, saying, "Papa, I love painting. I want to paint." But her father insisted that she stop. Yani broke into tears and told

Beautiful Lotus Pond
Age 7
2 × 17 ft.
Yani remembers the lotus pond in front of her home in Gongcheng.

Yani and her father at home.

her father that more than anything she wanted to keep on painting. Just then, he was called out of the room.

When her father returned with a friend, he was surprised to see that the whole floor was covered with Yani's paintings, each done in all seriousness. Yani looked up with tears in her eyes and said, "I can never paint again. These are my last works."

Her father said, "You have already apologized by words. And the paintings on the floor show you realize the mistake you have made." He told Yani that now she could continue to paint.

Wang Shiqiang's friend said to him, "You are really too strict with your daughter. But you are right. We must be strict with child prodigies who have won a name for themselves."

In 1985, when Yani was ten years old, she was interviewed by some sixty reporters in a big Tokyo hotel. One reporter asked, "We in Japan regard you as a great talent. How do you feel about that?"

"I feel nothing special," answered Yani, amid the flashes and clicks of cameras.

"Are your paintings the best in the world?"

"No," answered Yani. "If mine are, what about the works of other famous artists?"

6

Daily Life and Life on Tour

Yani and her family have now moved to Guilin, a city in the Guangxi Zhuang Autonomous Region. They have a more modern, spacious house than the one she grew up in, but Yani says she would rather live in the countryside of Gongcheng where there are mountains, rivers, and fields. She loves these mountains and rivers, which seem to belong to her, whereas the city of Guilin, though beautiful, belongs to the people. Her father says that maybe some day they will live in Gongcheng again.

Yani goes to school in Guilin until about four or five in the afternoon. After school she plays basketball, Ping-Pong, or goes jogging with her friends. Then she returns home to paint. It takes her about 30 to 40 minutes to paint each picture.

Yani has attended the opening ceremonies of

Yani and her father in Guilin.

Yani traveled to England in 1988 for an exhibition of her paintings.

A Dream of the Lijiang River
Age 13
2 ft. 2 in. × 2 ft. 3 in.
*Yani still prefers the countryside to
cities. This painting shows a
beautiful area of Guilin.*

her exhibitions in many parts of the world. She has traveled to many Chinese cities and toured countries in Asia, Europe, and North America. While traveling, she has tried to do as much sight-seeing as possible. She has been to Disneyland in Tokyo, visited museums in London, and the National Zoological Park in Washington. She has also visited many cities in Germany, beaches in California, and Japan's Mount Fuji. Touring has given Yani much stimulation for her painting, and she has done many paintings while on tour. Yani always carries her paints and brushes and paper wherever she goes, for she paints in her spare time, even on trains. But she finds being on tour very difficult.

When she is touring, she is always surrounded by reporters, with all their questions. She says she prefers a quieter life, with more time for painting. She looks forward to having time to herself so that she can do things on her own, rather than having everything arranged for her. And, she says, she would like to see more of the countryside wherever she goes, to see animals, mountains, and fields.

When Yani is away for a long time, she misses her family and wants to get home. The painting *Homesick* was done one night when she remembered a poem written by an ancient Chinese poet, Li Bai.

> *The white moonlight pours into my room,*
> *I take it for frost;*
> *Looking up at the moon in the sky,*
> *I think of my hometown.*

Yani painted *At My Friend's Home* in San Francisco. She must have been thinking of her own home in China when she painted it. She says that in the picture the monkey and chicks are playing

Opposite:
Impression of Red Roofs in West Germany
Age 10
1 ft. 6 in. × 2 ft. 3 in.
Yani paints when she's on tour. These are some buildings she saw when she was in Frankfurt.

Below: Yani skiing in Germany.

Homesick
Age 13
1 ft.2 in. × 2 ft. 6 in.
When she's away
from home for a
long time Yani misses
her family and friends
and the countryside
of China.

Snow
Age 12
3 ft. 2 in. × 5 ft. 10 in.
*(Painted in London.) Yani had
never seen snow before she went
to England.*

together. After a while, a mother hen wants her chicks to go home with her, but the chicks don't want to go. So, the monkey gets some rope and pretends it is an earthworm, which chicks like to eat. The monkey pulls the rope along the ground, and the chicks follow it all the way home!

Yani is not tutored when she is on tour, but when she goes back to China, her teachers help her catch up on her work. Her father has also arranged for her to have English lessons at home.

Yani does other things in her spare time as well as paint. She loves reading Chinese literature, listening to music, and playing musical instruments. She also writes poetry and prose, and she sings and dances. Although she is not an expert singer or dancer, she is far more than a beginner. And Yani still loves sports.

7
Growing and Changing

According to Chinese custom, a child becomes a youth at the age of fifteen. Yani has now said farewell to childhood.

Some people worry that gifted child painters will lose their innocence and imagination as they grow up and that they may not be able to paint any more noteworthy works. It is true that some young artists do lose their ability to create lively works, and some even give up painting entirely.

However, this is not true for Yani, for she has made a smooth transition from childhood to young adulthood. Her work continues to change and develop as she grows and changes. Though her work is no longer childlike — she paints fewer monkeys, and they no longer dominate her paintings — her subject matter has broadened and her brushwork has maintained vigor. In fact, it is becoming more skillful. Her paintings are becoming more mature, richer, and deeper, mingling fantasy with reality and expressing her individuality and inner self. Now she is showing a greater interest in flowers, mountains, brooks, people, birds, fish and other creatures.

Yani is in front of the flower beds at the Confucian temple in Gongcheng.

Note from the Seaside, painted when she was almost fifteen, is an example of her growth. It shows some little birds flying toward an old green tree by the sea. There is a sharp contrast between motion and stillness, and a combination of what is old with what is young. The tree trunk is painted with a powerful brushsweep, and the birds are depicted by soft dippings of light ink. This work shows that Yani has emerged from childhood into a new stage of development.

Her painting *I Can Smell the Fragrance* was painted when she was thirteen, but even though

Happy Spring Festival
Age 13
1 ft. 5 in. × 1 ft. 6 in.
The Spring Festival is a major celebration in China when people wear new clothes and buy gifts for each other.

it has a feeling of scribbling, it is different from her childhood works. Executed in a few strokes, the painting, though seemingly not complete, suggests awakening birds, cooling breezes, and the approach of spring. Her enthusiasm shows through, and it is clear that she is moving to a higher stage of development.

Yani stopped playing with monkeys long ago.

In recent years, she has also lost interest in fairy tales. But she is still painting freely, and she is still not tied to any one artistic style. In fact, the more she travels the more she uses different styles. Some of her paintings are impressionist in feeling, some have more of a scribble effect, some are done according to geometric rules, some have a rustic flavor, and some are more controlled. In this way, Yani

Picture for the Year of the Horse
Age 13
1 ft. 6 in. × 1 ft. 6 in.
In China, each new year is given the name of an animal. The animal is chosen from a list of twelve in sequence.

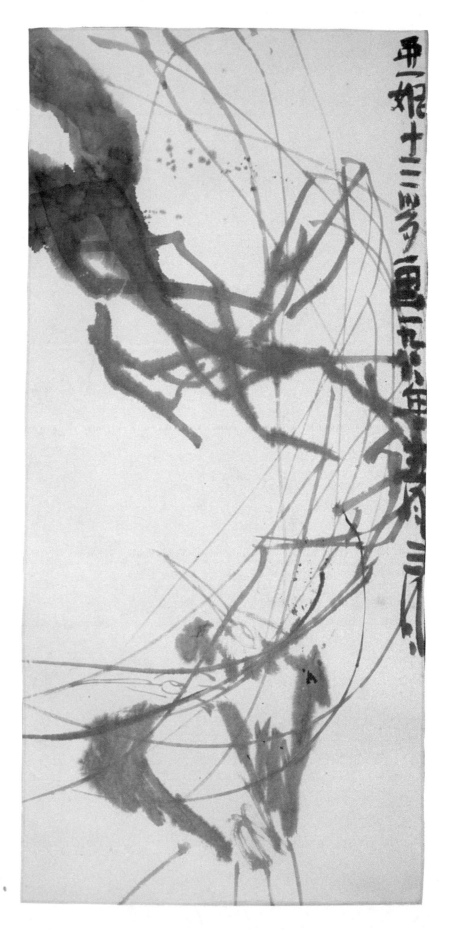

I Can Smell the Fragrance
Age 13
1 ft. 5 in. × 3 ft. 2 in.
*Yani painted this picture with just
a few brushstrokes.*

Remembering the Forest Where
I've Been
Age 13
1 ft. 3 in. × 1 ft. 5 in.

Yani likes to paint in a forest west of Guilin. The red house in the painting is a real house in the forest where some people live.

Above:
Notes from the Seaside
Age 14
3 ft. 2 in. × 5 ft. 10 in.
(Painted in San Francisco.) Yani combines powerful brushstrokes with soft dippings of light ink.

Right:
A Happy Episode
Age 13
1 ft. 7 in. × 2 ft. 2 in.

has proven herself different from other child prodigies, for many teenage prodigies excel in just one style.

To become a mature artist, Yani's father feels that a prodigy must have not only great intelligence, but also enthusiasm, will power and determination, ambition, creativity, originality, and confidence. Yani has all these qualities. In the future, her soul — her inner being — and her creativity must be protected, so that she can continue to paint spontaneously, expressing her joy, anger, and sorrow. And she must continue to have training in her thinking,

Rabbits and Butterfly
Age 13
1 ft. 3 in. × 1 ft. 7 in.
Rabbits mean something special to Yani because according to the Chinese calendar of years, she was born in the Year of the Rabbit.

64

Above:
Plum Blossoms in the New Year
Age 15
3 ft. 3 in. × 6 ft. 6 in.
Yani painted this for the new year 1991.

gain wide knowledge, and have rich experiences in life in order to realize her full potential.

According to Jan Stuart, Yani is a riddle. "She defies us," she says. "We are always charting influences from the past, but with Yani, such influences do not exist."

And, to Zhang Ting, a famous Chinese art critic, Yani has achieved what some artists have failed to do in a lifetime.

Yani is already a national treasure. One day she may become one of the great Chinese painters of her time.

Afterword

When I first met Yani, she was only five years old. That day she sat on the floor in my sitting room and painted on a piece of *xuan* paper larger than herself. With a big brush in her hand, she painted a picture of a lotus pond. Next to it, a little monkey sat looking up at the sky. Yani was painting herself, I thought at the time.

Now, ten years later, Yani has made great progress. She has held solo exhibitions of her paintings not only in China but also in Great Britain, the United States, Japan, and Germany.

Like every child, Yani has inborn gifts. However, for Yani the most important thing is that her gifts have been well protected and developed. Whether she can continue to be a fine painter in the future depends on herself, because other personal traits are vital, too—diligence, persistence, honesty, responsibility, and initiative.

Yani's future path is bright and promising. Yani, just go ahead.

Sha Hong, Deputy Counselor of the
China Personnel Research Society,
Vice-Chairman of the China Research
Society of Oriental Culture

Yani in front of her painting
Plum Blossoms in the New Year.

Traditional Chinese Painting

by Zheng Zhensun and Alice Low

The Tools

A selection of traditional Chinese art materials.

Different types of Chinese brushes showing varying thicknesses.

Though Yani's painting is highly individual, her technique is influenced by that of traditional Chinese painting, which developed gradually over many centuries. Traditional Chinese painting stresses brush and ink techniques, and this is one of the main ways that it differs from painting in much of the West, such as Europe and the United States.

The traditional Chinese painter uses special writing brushes, inks, and paper, as well as different pigments, which make the colors of traditional Chinese painting distinct.

There are three types of Chinese brushes: stiff-haired, soft fleece, and another kind, which is neither too soft, nor too stiff.

The stiff brush is made of animal hair, mainly that of a weasel, combined with badger hair, marten hair, and short pig bristles. The artist uses the stiff brush to give an effect of strength and liveliness.

The soft brush is made mainly of fleece, with the addition of birds' feathers.

The third kind of brush is made of both stiff hairs and soft fleece. It is a mixture of soft fleece and weasel hair, or soft fleece and rabbit hair. The artist chooses this kind of brush for the combined effect of strength and grace.

Brushes for painting come in three sizes—large, medium, and small.

In the past, the traditional Chinese painter used an inkstick of black solid pigment, and an inkslab, a stone on which to grind the inkstick. When artists used ink for painting, they would grind a dry inkstick on an inkslab dampened with water to get black liquid ink. Ink black is the basic color used in Chinese painting. Nowadays, it is no longer necessary to grind the inkstick, for prepared ink is available.

Yani's inkstick and inkslab.

There are several kinds of ink: Many people use tong oil soot-ink, which is both black and bright.

Most traditional Chinese painters like to paint on *xuan* paper, which is handmade from rice straw, the bark of a special kind of tree, and other vegetable fibers. *Xuan* paper absorbs moisture, and the ink and colors sink in easily when water is added. When painters paint on this paper, they can produce many shades of ink and color, using a variety of brushstrokes.

Yani grinds the inkstick on the dampened inkslab to make liquid ink.

The effects produced by artists using these brushes, ink, and paper give traditional Chinese painting its special look and feel.

Xuan paper can also be treated so that it changes to absorb less moisture; therefore, ink and colors do not sink in as much. When Chinese painters want to paint layers of colors, they use *xuan* paper that has been treated in this special way.

Pigments for the colors used in traditional Chinese painting are made from minerals or plants. Mineral pigments are thick and opaque, and plant pigments are thin and transparent. Recently, artists have been able to buy synthetic pigments. They come in tubes, much like toothpaste.

Left: Tubes of pigment.
Right: Prepared ink.

Two Styles of Painting

Traditional Chinese painting is divided into two major schools: *gongbi hua*, an elegant, detailed style, and *xieyi hua*, a free style, which is bolder and

68

more lively. All of Yani's paintings are done in the *xieyi hua* style, and using it, she captures the form and spirit, ideas and feeling of an object in concise strokes.

Figure painting; landscape painting; and flower, bird, and animal painting are the three subjects painted by traditional Chinese painters.

Traditional Chinese painting tries to capture the idea or spirit of what the artist sees and feels, rather than just copying what something looks like.

For instance, some artists prefer to show the pine tree as a "warrior" who braves the wind and snow, rather than portraying it simply as an evergreen. Or if an artist wants to paint a lotus flower, there are many choices as to how the artist may want the flower to look and seem. One artist might want to emphasize the many petals and the rich fragrance so the viewer can almost smell it; another artist might want to bring out the quiet elegance of one lotus blossom blooming by itself; another might want to stress its beautiful color.

In addition, traditional Chinese painting does not usually concern itself with perspective; rather, it concentrates on the arrangement of black or colored areas, and areas that are left blank. If the painting has too many brushstrokes and objects, it would seem too solid and not airy enough.

Using Brushes and Ink

In traditional Chinese painting, there are certain ways to hold the brush and to wield it, as well as certain brush and ink techniques.

When holding the brush, you should keep your fingers firm and your palm relaxed. The thumb, index and third fingers hold the brush firmly, while the fourth and pinky fingers help support the

Detail from Beautiful Lotus Pond. *Yani shows the colors of lotus flowers.*

Left:
Going to Play with
the Monkey
Age 10
3 ft. 2 in. × 5 ft. 10 in.
The inscription reads:
"One day, three big tigers
go down the mountain
to play with the little
monkey." Yani has been
more concerned with
space than with per-
spective in this painting.

Opposite:
Welcoming the Year
of the Rabbit
Age 11
1 ft. 10 in. × 2 ft. 9 in.
Yani captures the
happy feeling of this
occasion in her painting.

brush. There should be enough space between your fingers and the brush for you to wield the brush with ease. However, Yani holds her brush in the way that is most comfortable for her, rather than sticking to the traditional method.

The way you move your brush depends on the size of the painting you are working on. Usually, if you are working on a small painting, you will use your fingers and wrists more. If you are working on a large painting, you will use your arm and even the upper part of your body to make your brushstrokes. Whether you are painting a large picture or a small one, it is very important to coordinate your fingers, wrist, and arm.

There are various ways of using the brush tip. You may use the brush tip in a forward direction or backward direction, in a single stroke or scattered

In November 1989 Yani painted a huge painting in the Confucian temple in Gongcheng. The photographs show how Yani painted the picture.

1. Calm thoughts before making the first brushstroke.

2. Inspiration comes when the brush is full of ink.

3. Dividing up the blank paper with outlines.

72

strokes, or by turning or twisting the brush. You may use the brush tip lightly or heavily, depending on whether you lift it or press it. You may also use your brush quickly or slowly. Your brushstrokes will produce different effects if they are angular or smooth, flowing or awkward, vigorous or graceful, heavy or light.

There are many other brush techniques. *Plain line drawing* to make outlines is the basis of traditional Chinese painting. It has a powerful expressive feeling, and you can draw objects in this way alone without using shading or color.

Cun, or texture strokes, is used to show the rugged surface of rock and can produce their characteristic shapes and feeling. The word *cun* means wrinkles on the skin caused by cold wind blowing.

Ca, or rubbing, is used along with *cun* texture

4. *Branches and leaves are painted using bold lines.*

5. *Standing on the painting to reach the top of the paper.*

painting. For example, in making texture strokes to paint rocks, your brush can be full of ink and produce clear brush touches, or you can use a brush that is dry so your touches are indistinct. In these kinds of texture strokes the brush is used to rub horizontally.

Dotting is another brushstroke technique, and it is the opposite of contouring, or bold line drawing. Tiny plants, grass, and leaves are all painted with dots. Dotting is often used in painting portraits, flowers, and birds in a free style. Yani paints most of her small birds using this dotting technique.

There are several ways of using ink to produce a wide range of gradations and various effects. In the *jimo* technique, ink is applied from light to dark and built up gradually. First, a painter uses light ink as the base. After it is dry, the painter adds a

Detail from Notes from the Seaside
Yani painted these birds using the dotting technique.

6. *Left: Painting thick and thin lines.*

7. *Above: Thinking about what has been painted so far and what to paint next.*

second layer and then the third, so that the layers do not mix with each other.

In the *pomo* technique, the ink looks as though it had been splashed on the paper. Paintings with bold and free strokes are often done with this *pomo* technique. When the painter finds that the ink shade already painted is not satisfactory, he or she adds some heavy or light ink. This is called the *poumo* technique. This ink and wash style of painting makes light and heavy inks mix with each other to produce a fresh, vivid look.

Traditional Chinese painters also use other special skills, such as painting after rubbing or wrinkling the paper, painting on paper with something put underneath it, or spraying the paper with water before painting. These skills create other effects.

8. Above: Painting the first monkey using light brushstrokes.

9. Right: Moving to the bottom of the painting to add more monkeys.

Inscriptions and Seals

Often, there are inscriptions on traditional Chinese paintings, but not every painting must have an inscription. Inscriptions vary, depending on the painter's feeling about a particular painting, or depending on the personality of the painter.

Some painters write only their names on the paintings; others like to add the date and the place of where the painting was done. Some write the title of the painting, and some even include a poem, a short essay, or even notes about the story or idea in the painting. Yani often puts inscriptions on her paintings, such as *Animals' Autumn*. Here, the inscription reads, "Autumn seems to be a withering season for trees, but the animals are happy." Yani says that animals love

10. *Adding more ink.*   11. *Giving a red outline to a basket.*

Some of Yani's seals and the red ink paste that is used to stamp with.

Yani's seal

autumn because they can find lots of fruit to eat.

A painter thinks carefully about where to put the inscription, as well as deciding what size and shape seals to use. A seal is like a signature and may be square, round, oblong, or even irregular in shape. Seals have Chinese characters (words) on them, and they are carved in relief so that the artist can stamp them on the painting. Yani takes a great deal of care over how and where she uses her seals on her paintings.

Many traditional Chinese painters emphasize careful observation, so that they can paint from memory. Yani excels at this. Although traditional Chinese painters also sketch directly from real life, Yani does not make sketches before she paints. Like some other traditional Chinese artists, she paints boldly and without hesitation.

12. Above: Adding the seal after painting the inscription.

13. Right: Judging what has been done. Yani called the painting On the Way Home. *It measured 3 feet by 5 feet and 10 inches.*

Glossary of Chinese terms

Beijing *(baijing)*
The capital city of the People's Republic of China.

Ca *(tsa)*
Rubbing; a technique used in Chinese art to produce textured brushstrokes.

Chaijiang *(chajiang)*
A river located in Gongcheng County.

Cun *(tsun)*
A brushstroke technique used in Chinese art; literally means 'wrinkles on the skin caused by the cold wind blowing.'

Erhu *(as it reads)*
A Chinese string instrument.

Gongbi hua *(as it reads)*
One of the schools of traditional Chinese painting; an elegant, detailed style of painting.

Gongcheng *(as it reads)*
Yani's hometown in the Guangxi Zhuang Autonomous Region.

Guangxi Zhuang *(guangchi juang)*
An autonomous region in southern China.

Guangzhou *(gwangjo)*
A port city in southeast China.

Guilin *(gweilin)*
A city and mountainous region of the Guangxi Zhuang Autonomous Region.

Jimo *(as it reads)*
Art technique using ink to gradually build up shades from light to dark.

Li Bai *(as it reads)*
Ancient Chinese poet who lived 701-762 CE.

Lida *(as it reads)*
The name of Wang Yani's pet monkey.

Nanning *(as it reads)*
Capital city of the Guangxi Zhuang Autonomous Region.

Pomo *(as it reads)*
Art technique using ink where the ink is splashed on the paper.

Poumo *(as it reads)*
Art technique adding heavy or light ink on another ink wash to produce the correct shade; an ink and wash style of painting.

Qufu *(chufu)*
City in the Shandong Province of China.

Shandong *(as it reads)*
Province located in eastern China.

Shanghai *(as it reads)*
Port city in eastern China.

Shiyan *(as it reads)*
Wang Yani's elementary school; literally 'experimental.'

Taishan (*as it reads*)
Mountain range in the Shandong Province.

Tang Fengjiao (*as it reads*)
Wang Yani's mother.

Wang Shiqiang (*wang shichiang*)
Wang Yani's father.

Wang Xiangyu (*wang shangyu*)
Wang Yani's brother.

Wang Yani (*as it reads*)

Xieyi hua (*shiyi hua*)
One of the schools of traditional Chinese painting; a free, bold style of painting.

Xuan (*chewan*)
Chinese art paper made from vegetable fibers.

Yangzhou (*yangjo*)
City in eastern China.

Zhang Ting (*jang ting*)
Chinese art critic.

Map of the People's Republic of China showing the Guangxi Zhuang Autonomous Region.

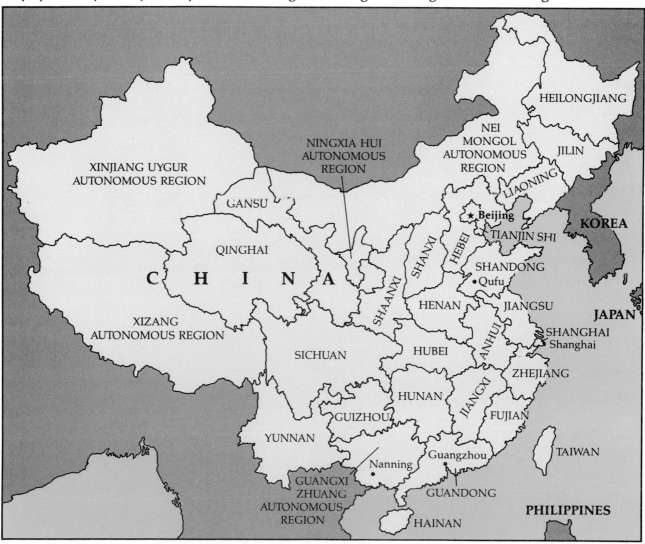

Index

Animals in Art

by Marjorie Jackson

*T*hroughout the ages, artists have been fascinated by animals, trying to portray them in various poses, shapes and forms. Some painters, like the German Albrecht Dürer, concentrate on the natural characteristics of an animal, making it seem as real as possible, ready to leap from the canvas. Others emphasize what the animal means to them, as Picasso does with his fierce rooster; still others try to convey what they admire or fear about the creature. But all artists who portray animals have one thing in common—they hope to capture the animal's nature in their work, bringing its unique spirit to life through paint, clay, stone, or metal.

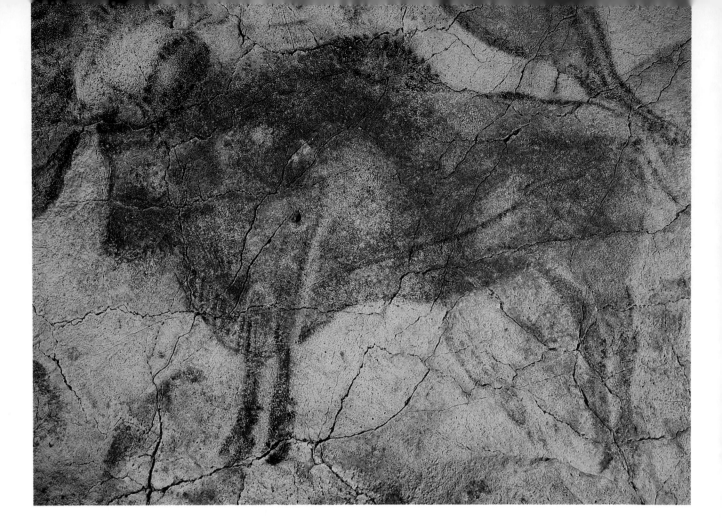

Ice Age Bison

20,000–15,000 years ago, Spain

Thousands of years ago, Ice Age artists crawled down dark tunnels to secret caverns where they carved and painted herds of animals. Bison, horses, antelopes, and other creatures still race across the rough walls and ceilings. Prehistoric artists made their paints by grinding soil and rocks and adding animal fat and water or urine. They used hair and bristle brushes, hollow bird-bone blowing tubes, and fur "sponges" to apply the color. The paintings, hidden deep underground, may have been part of special ceremonial rites believed to bring success in the hunt or to cause herds to multiply.

Antelope and Lion Playing Senet
1200s–1100s B.C., Egypt

This ancient painting on papyrus shows animals behaving like human beings, much as they do in some modern cartoon strips. The artist outlined the animals' shapes and painted them in tawny colors. The animals' eyes are brightly outlined, too, just as Egyptian men and women rimmed theirs with black kohl. The unlikely companions—after all, lions *eat* antelopes—are playing senet, a popular board game of the time, similar to backgammon.

Rhinoceros Tsun
1000s B.C., China

Two-horned rhinoceroses still roamed in southern China when an artist shaped this *tsun*, a ceremonial wine vessel, by pouring liquid bronze into a clay mold. The stance of the rhino's legs and its forward-thrusting head give a real sense of animal power, but the overround eyes and body and flapping ears make it seem playful. Chinese writing inside the body tells the story of the vessel. A man named Yü had won a great battle, and the king rewarded him with cowrie shells, the money of that time. Yü spent the shells for this tsun.

Scythian Stag

late 600s–early 500s B.C., Siberia

Scythians were warrior-nomads who roamed throughout Europe and Central Asia, driving great herds of cattle and horses before them. This twelve-inch-long gilt-bronze stag once decorated a chieftain's iron shield. The Scythians valued the stag's speed and strength in fighting, and the chieftain hoped, by holding its image in battle, to gain these powers for himself. Nomads must carry their riches with them, and the chieftain took the stag with him to his grave in Siberia, where it was found by archeologists.

Sea
Creature
Parade
300s B.C., Italy

The potter who made this
ceramic plate showed the special traits
of sea creatures. At the top, the bright spots of an
electric eel warn of danger—the fish can produce
enough electricity to stun a human! Left, an octopus
lurks, a myriad of suckers shown along its legs. At
the bottom, a spotted skate swims with two mackerels.
Its spots are camouflage, for blending with sand and
rocks on the ocean floor. Right, a streamlined, bright-
eyed squid streaks upward. The smaller creatures are
shellfish.

In spite of the potter's careful attention to detail, there
are two mistakes on the plate. Can you find them?

Dürer's Hare

A.D. 1502, Germany

Almost five hundred years ago, at a time when he was painting every-thing that "creepeth or flieth," the famous artist Albrecht Dürer created this crouching hare. Dürer worked from a live model so that he could catch every detail, such as the long, wavy ears, twitchy whiskers, and soft fur. He placed the hare alone on the page for importance and used a fine-tipped brush to draw attention to every hair in its coat. No one has ever painted a more true-to-life animal.

Friendly Tiger

1800s, Korea

Fierce tigers once roamed Korea, and natu-rally people were afraid. But artists soon tamed the roaring tiger by making it look foolish. It was given a leopard-spotted head, a tiger-striped body, the stance of a pussycat with feet too big and clumsy for a chase, and a silly, toothy grin. Even the tiny magpie isn't afraid to scold such a tiger.

Picasso's Rooster
1938, Spain

In the past, many people believed that a rooster's morning crow drove the darkness away. When Pablo Picasso drew his rooster, his homeland was being destroyed by war. *Wake up!* the animal seems to say to all free nations. It bristles with fierceness, its feathers ruffled, its beak sharp. Picasso painted a simple subject, but gave it a profound message.

Enchanted Owl
1960, Canadian Arctic

Kenojuak, an Inuit woman from Cape Dorset settlement, created this amazing bird. Inuit artists today combine ancient images and carving skills with modern printing methods to produce wildly free works. Kenojuak's owl is both natural and fantastic—its eyes stare and its claws cling like those of a real owl, but the striking whirl of feathers gives a sense of awesome power. With great patience, the artist worked this design into a stone slab, chipping away the unwanted parts. The printer then carefully applied two colors to the stone, making the light seem to push away the darkness. Kenojuak has signed in Inuit syllabic at lower right, and the printer's signature is beneath; the small igloo shape at the bottom is for Cape Dorset.

Ferdinand (A Horse)
1990, United States

The sculptor Deborah Butterfield made Ferdinand of chunks of scrap steel, including an F-, a C-, and a V-shape. She welded large pieces for the torso and haunches and strips of metal for additional lines. The open spaces draw the viewer's eye into the intricate interior of the horse. Butterfield rides and trains horses in her free time and uses her intimate knowledge of them to create graceful, natural stances and postures. But each new sculpture is still hard work until a sense of life comes into it, until it reflects the image she holds in her mind of "horse."

Animal Scribbles

Gesture Drawings

Animals are fun to draw, but it can be hard to use a real animal as a model because they're always moving. To make realistic animal drawings, artists first make scribble drawings called *gesture drawings*. Doing gesture drawings of animals is a fast way of making sketches. All you have to do is make your scribbles look like the outline and main shapes of the animal. Don't bother with details, just scribble. Study what your animal looks like—then draw fast! It's fun to make lots of gesture drawings.

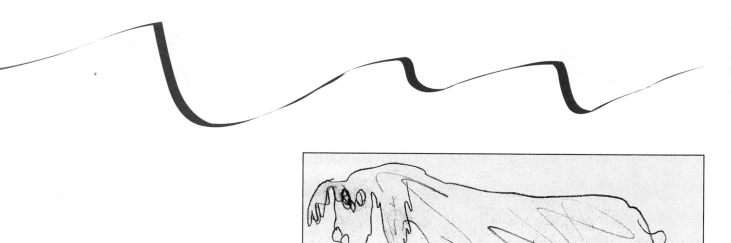

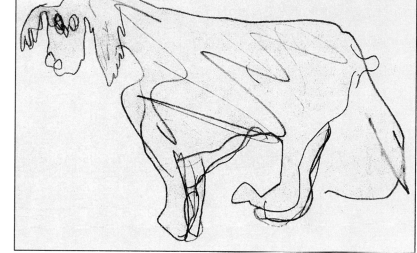

Start with an animal that's asleep. Then try doing a scribble while the animal is moving. Work fast! Your sketches don't have to be big and you can do one in less than a minute.

Pick one of your best scribbles to work on to make a finished drawing. Erase lines that you don't like. Draw heavier lines on top. Add eyes and whiskers; draw texture lines to show fur or feathers.

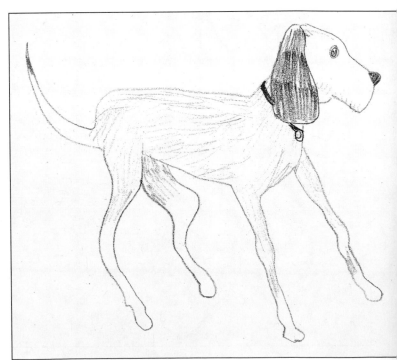

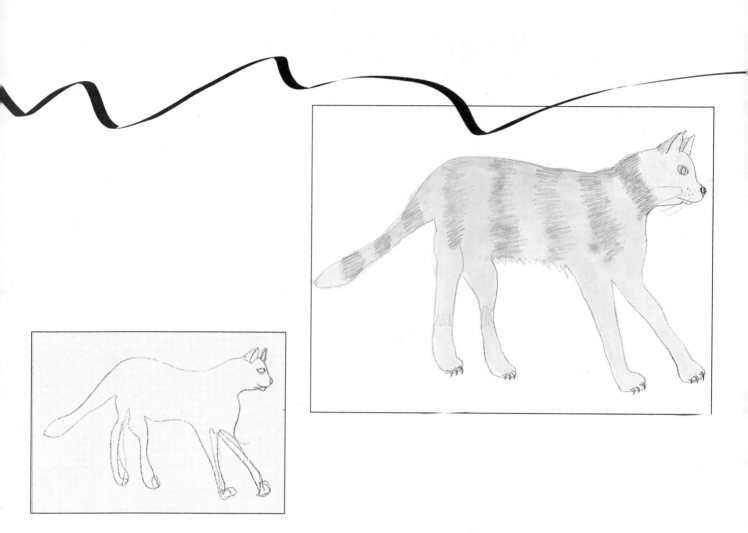

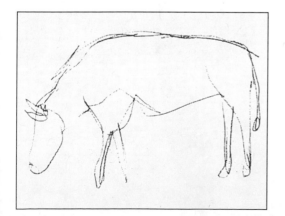

Add color or try drawing with a paintbrush and watery black paint. It's easy to make a great animal picture when you start with a scribble!

Pen and Ink on Vellum

Pastel
on Paper

Create
Your Own
Masterpiece

These are some of the
materials you might use to
make your own work of art.

Charcoal
on Paper

Watercolor
on Paper

Colored
Pencils
on Paper

Oil Paint on Canvas

94